ST. NICHOLAS

AND THE VALLEY BEYOND

AND THE VALLEY BEYOND

A CHRISTMAS LEGEND

WRITTEN BY

Ellen Kushner

CREATED AND PAINTED BY

Richard W. Burhans

BASED ON AN ORIGINAL STORY BY

**Virginia Burhans Sturm, Sallie P. Burhans,
and Richard W. Burhans**

VIKING STUDIO BOOKS
Published by the Penguin Group
Penguin Books USA Inc., 375 Hudson Street,
New York, New York 10014, U.S.A.
Penguin Books Ltd, 27 Wrights Lane,
London W8 5TZ, England
Penguin Books Australia Ltd, Ringwood,
Victoria, Australia
Penguin Books Canada Ltd, 10 Alcorn Avenue,
Toronto, Ontario, Canada M4V 3B2
Penguin Books (N.Z.) Ltd, 182–190 Wairau Road,
Auckland 10, New Zealand

Penguin Books Ltd, Registered Offices:
Harmondsworth, Middlesex, England

First published in 1994 by Viking Penguin,
a division of Penguin Books USA Inc.

1 2 3 4 5 6 7 8 9 10

ISBN 0-670-84420-9

Library of Congress
Cataloging-in-Publication Data available

Printed in Italy
Set in Post Antiqua
Photography for color separations of original
oil paintings produced by Dave Hagyard

Please address all correspondence to
St. Nick, Inc., P. O. Box 797
Snoqualmie, WA 98065

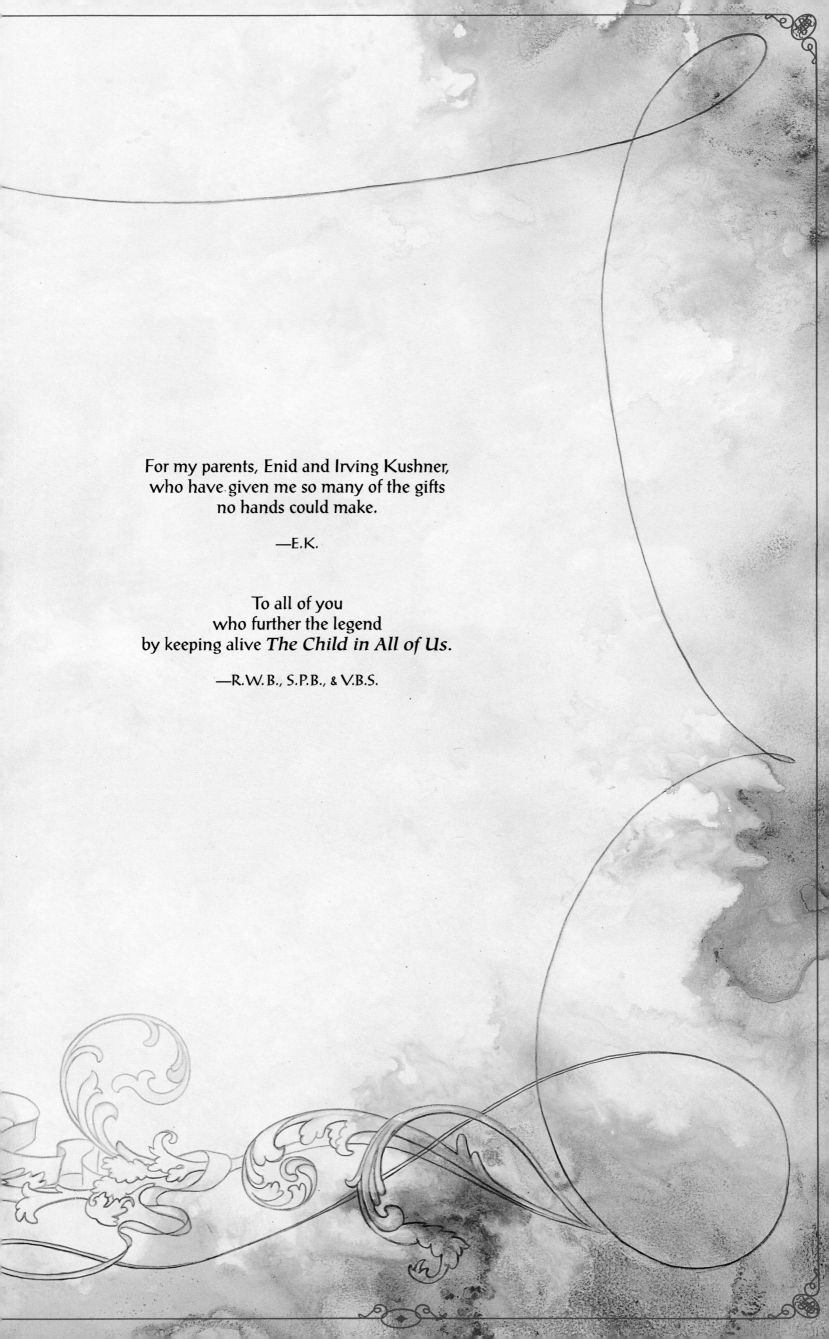

For my parents, Enid and Irving Kushner,
who have given me so many of the gifts
no hands could make.

—E.K.

To all of you
who further the legend
by keeping alive *The Child in All of Us*.

—R.W.B., S.P.B., & V.B.S.

ST. NICHOLAS

AND THE VALLEY BEYOND

THE VALLEY BEYOND

PLAYBILL

St. Nicholas

Wilhelmina

Woodshaper

Weaver

Baker

Beekeeper

Iron Former

Ice Skater

Light Maker

Master Carver

Logger

Homemaker

A
no hands
can make me
two hands
can shape me
all hands
can take me

It was a long, long time ago, and he was a poor boy on a cold, cold night. No one came out of the warm houses to give him food or invite him in to sit by the fire. All he could do was walk and walk, trying to keep warm. All the nights he could remember were cold and lonely. The boy was very young.

He was afraid to stop for fear that someone would hurl harsh words at him or even kick him and tell him to move along. And so he walked on, until the houses were left behind. It was a clear night, and the stars seemed very cold and far away. He was alone, except for the wind and the stars and the distant hills. He thought, It will always be this way. And he wanted to lie down and give in to the cold and the loneliness.

But there was a voice in his head saying, "Keep going. Keep walking." It was the sort of voice he'd always imagined but could barely remember having heard, a voice full of kindness, a voice that lived in warmth and light. He looked around, but saw no one. The night was darker. With the kind voice in his head, the boy kept walking.

As he walked, he began to grow warmer. It was as if someone were wrapping him in fur, breathing words of comfort in his ear: "Welcome, welcome, young friend!"

He saw nothing. He walked in a thick mist. Then, slowly, ahead of him, a great light began to glow. And with it, the boy saw that he was not alone at all—on either side of him, four-legged beasts paced with graceful majesty, like the honor guard for a prince.

The path grew steeper. The boy nearly fell, but his guides gave him their strength, guiding him along until they had come to the top.

The boy looked and saw what they meant him to see: in the light of a warm and beaming moon, a great valley spread out before him, surrounded by mountains like dragons' teeth; and nestled in its bottom a golden village glittered.

The valley was like nothing he had ever seen before. He'd never heard any travelers' tales of such a place: warm and welcoming in the midst of the lonely mountains. It burned the cold spot in the boy's heart. Why had his guides brought him here to show him yet another place where everyone was happy but him?

"Child," they said, "here is your home." And they nuzzled him with their warm noses, gazed at him with their warm eyes: "Go down," they said. "Don't be afraid."

He began running down the mountain toward the light. With every step he felt stronger and taller and freer.

In the village, he followed the sound of music and laughter to a glorious ballroom.

People seized both his hands and whirled him into the dance. And soon he was laughing with them, and he knew that he was home.

After the dance, there was a warm fire, and food to eat and hot mead to drink. He ate and drank more than he ever had in his life. But when a pretty young woman offered him a handsomely carved pipe to smoke, he laughed: "I'm just a child! I can't smoke a pipe!"

"Don't be silly," she said with a smile. "You're a fine young man."

She had such a nice face, he couldn't believe her smile could hide a cruel heart. "Stop making fun of me."

"But you are," she said. "A fine man. The finest I have ever seen." And then she became shy and looked the other way.

The funny thing was, when he looked down at himself, he found that it was true. His legs were long, his arms were strong. He was no longer a little child.

He felt as if he could reach for the moon and pluck it right out of the sky. "I've done it!" he shouted. "No one will ever hurt me again! I was little and alone, so people said I would surely starve or freeze to death and never live to grow up. But I've done it, I've grown up! I've escaped!"

"Goodness," said the girl, "where do you come from? It sounds like a terrible place, with all this starving and freezing."

His face darkened when he thought of it. "What does it matter where I'm from? It's the same everywhere."

"Not here," she said. "Not in the Valley Beyond the World's Edge. Here there is no hunger, and no loneliness."

"No hunger and no loneliness," he repeated in a voice of wonder. "But what do you do?"

"We make things," the girl replied. "We work with our hands and hearts and minds. We work in shape and color, in wood and wool, with wax and needle and flax and flame. And each one helps their neighbor, or how can things get done?"

He said, "I think I like it here."

"I think I like *you*, too. What's your name?"

"It's Nicholas."

"Mine's Wilhelmina," she said. "But it's such a mouthful. Everyone calls me Willie. And I will call you Nick. Do you mind?"

He did not mind at all.

The people of the Valley made the young man welcome. They treated him more like a long-lost brother than a stranger.

At first, Nick wanted to talk about the fear and hunger he remembered in the world he had left behind. But when he spoke of these things to his new friends, they looked so confused. Hearing about so much misery made them unhappy. Soon he stopped talking about it. And as time went on, he even stopped thinking about it . . . until Nick began to forget. The fears of his childhood became a memory, and then a dream, and then not even that, until even Nick himself came to believe that, like everyone else, he had always lived in the Valley.

The years went by, as years will, even in the Valley Beyond the World's Edge. Nick and Willie spent all of their time together, exploring the wonders of the Valley, swimming its rivers, climbing its hills, tromping through its forests. . . .

They came to know everyone in the Valley, from the woodsmen who brought the logs from the deep forests,

to the mill folk by the river who sawed them, to the carpenters in town who smoothed the wood down and the toymakers who carved it into cunning dolls and boats and whistles.

Nick and Willie knew the beekeepers who lived in the flowery meadows where the bees gathered honey among the towering foxglove, the rows of golden woad and nodding iris; bright marigold, delicate poppy and regal dahlias and sweet-smelling columbine; the fragrant lavender and the lilies.

hey knew the dye makers who used those same
flowers to bring forth colors to delight the eye,
pressing and pounding and boiling, soaking and
stirring until the bright petals released their colors
in strange and unexpected ways. In their
workshop the smell of flowers mingled with the acid smells of
root and mineral, and the rafters hung with drying plants and
great swoops of drying cloth.

And the two visited the candlemakers who took the bees'
wax and the dyers' colors and made of them a world of light.

In the weavers' workshop, Willie and Nick sat for hours among the spinning wheels and great-framed looms, lost in the hum of the wheels as the skilled hands of the women reeled off the bright threads of color the dyers had made, while from the looms the shuttles thrummed and battens thumped in steady counterpoint.

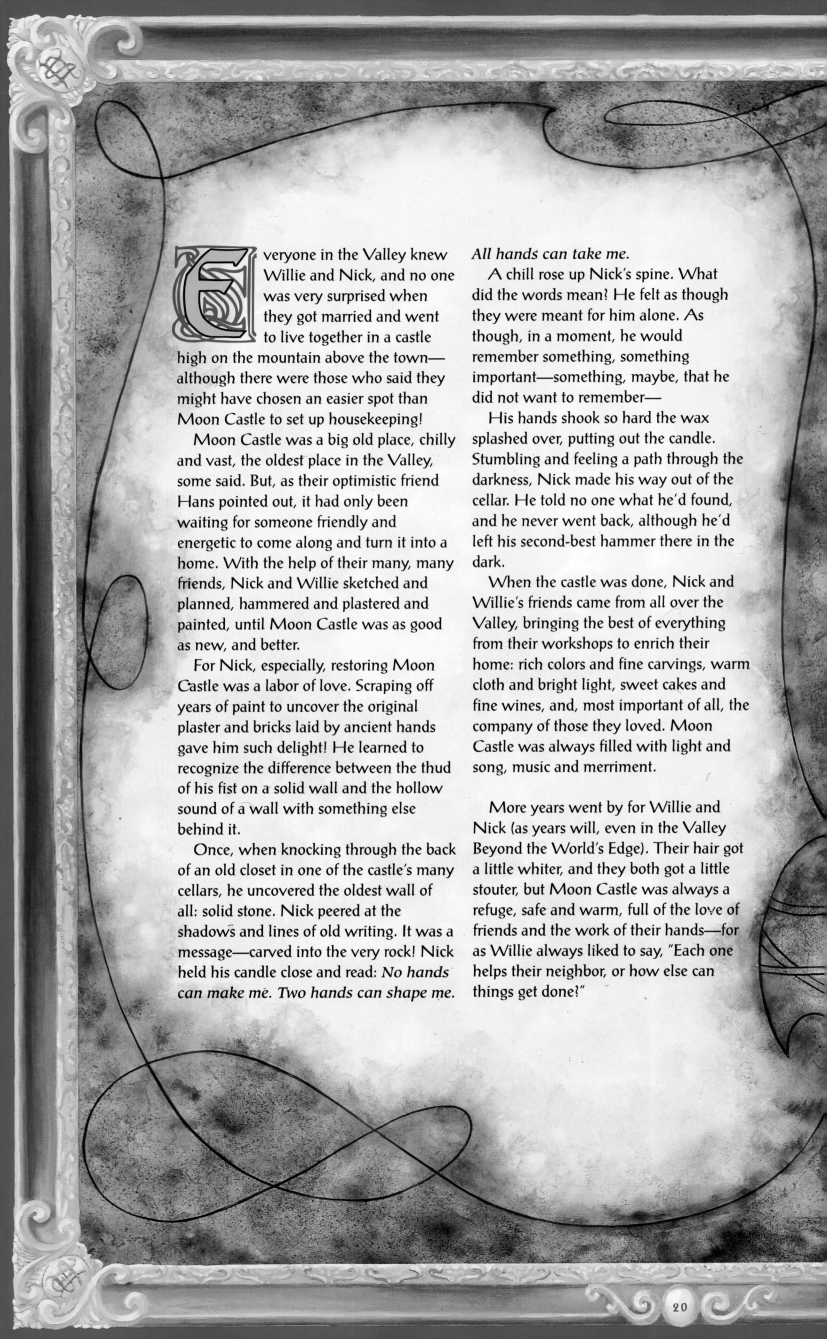

Everyone in the Valley knew Willie and Nick, and no one was very surprised when they got married and went to live together in a castle high on the mountain above the town—although there were those who said they might have chosen an easier spot than Moon Castle to set up housekeeping!

Moon Castle was a big old place, chilly and vast, the oldest place in the Valley, some said. But, as their optimistic friend Hans pointed out, it had only been waiting for someone friendly and energetic to come along and turn it into a home. With the help of their many, many friends, Nick and Willie sketched and planned, hammered and plastered and painted, until Moon Castle was as good as new, and better.

For Nick, especially, restoring Moon Castle was a labor of love. Scraping off years of paint to uncover the original plaster and bricks laid by ancient hands gave him such delight! He learned to recognize the difference between the thud of his fist on a solid wall and the hollow sound of a wall with something else behind it.

Once, when knocking through the back of an old closet in one of the castle's many cellars, he uncovered the oldest wall of all: solid stone. Nick peered at the shadows and lines of old writing. It was a message—carved into the very rock! Nick held his candle close and read: *No hands can make me. Two hands can shape me.*

All hands can take me.

A chill rose up Nick's spine. What did the words mean? He felt as though they were meant for him alone. As though, in a moment, he would remember something, something important—something, maybe, that he did not want to remember—

His hands shook so hard the wax splashed over, putting out the candle. Stumbling and feeling a path through the darkness, Nick made his way out of the cellar. He told no one what he'd found, and he never went back, although he'd left his second-best hammer there in the dark.

When the castle was done, Nick and Willie's friends came from all over the Valley, bringing the best of everything from their workshops to enrich their home: rich colors and fine carvings, warm cloth and bright light, sweet cakes and fine wines, and, most important of all, the company of those they loved. Moon Castle was always filled with light and song, music and merriment.

More years went by for Willie and Nick (as years will, even in the Valley Beyond the World's Edge). Their hair got a little whiter, and they both got a little stouter, but Moon Castle was always a refuge, safe and warm, full of the love of friends and the work of their hands—for as Willie always liked to say, "Each one helps their neighbor, or how else can things get done?"

Then, one night, Nick dreamed a dream.

It was a dream of hunger, a dream of cold, a dream of ice in the heart and fire in the bone. It was a dream of loneliness and helplessness, of fears without a name that were more powerful than any words that anyone could ever speak, or think, or hear.

Nick woke up in the darkness, and his hands shook until he found the light.

And there was his room, and there were his things, his pipes and his books, his boots and his charts, and his lovely Willie. Everything was where it should be.

But there, in the corner—was that darkness, still? Was it the fear without a name, waiting to come and get him?

In the morning, Willie said, "Whatever happened to you last night? You sat awake for hours, with all the candles lit."

"I had a dream," he answered. "And when I woke, still I could feel the darkness of the dream, waiting to come and get me."

She said, "I'll hold you tight, so tight the darkness will never find you."

But that night, Nick again dreamed of cold. He dreamed that the fire of the sun had gone away; even the light of the stars was hidden by the tall mountains, and all the Valley was covered with ice. He woke up shivering in Willie's arms.

Willie wrapped him in blankets, and built up the fire, and fed him spicy tea. But Nick was glad to see the sun rise and to feel the heat of the day come up on the mountain.

"There's something wrong," he kept saying, "something terribly wrong in the Valley."

"It was only a dream," she comforted him. "Just a bad dream." She felt his forehead. "Maybe you're coming down with something."

But in his heart he knew that it was more than that.

illie had never seen her Nick so deeply troubled. And for what! Only a dream. But nothing she said could make it any better. The thing was getting beyond her. Maybe, she thought, he's been spending too much time cooped up with me in this old castle. Maybe he needs to get away. She sent a message to some of their closest friends: a party—a picnic—anything to distract him and lift the shadow from his heart!

And so they came, riding up to Moon Castle in Otto's wonderful old oxcart. Willie dressed Nick in his warm red suit with the white fur trim, and kissed him, and made him promise to keep his hat on if it got cold. "Go on," she chided, "give me a chance to clean up your study without you getting in my way!"

Nick began to feel that things were not so ominous after all. How could they be, with the sun shining and his friends all around him, and Willie safe at home! There was no fear, no chill, no darkness. Jokes were told, and songs were sung, and they were very merry.

"Here's a good one for you!" cried Otto. "It's an old riddle they used to tell in my workshop: *No hands can make me. Two hands can shape me. All hands can take me. What am I?*"

The words had a strange effect on Nick: he jumped in his seat, nearly fell off the back of the oxcart. "Why, it's a riddle!" he exclaimed.

"I told you that," said Otto. "Don't look so startled, Nick—you look like you've seen a ghost. What's the matter?"

In his mind, Nick saw the carving on his cellar wall. Again, chilly fingers teased at his memory. And again, he pushed them away. "I'm no good at riddles," he said gruffly.

"Come on," cheerful Hans said. "It's easy! 'No hands can make me'—that's got to be a flower!"

"But two hands can't *shape* a flower, my friend!" argued Abe, the dye cutter.

"Hmm," said Leah, "how about wood? Two hands can shape wood into a lot of things."

"But what about 'All hands can take me'?"

"Hmm . . . that's tough," said Hans. "We give up, Otto. What is it?"

"Nothing."

"What?"

"Well," explained Otto, "no one's ever figured out the answer. It's called the Lost Riddle. Our old foreman used to say that someday, someone would come from beyond the World's Edge to solve it for us."

"That's a long way to come just to solve a riddle!" joked Hans.

But Otto wasn't smiling. "He said, when the riddle was solved, the Valley would be healed."

"But there's nothing *wrong* with the Valley!"

"And there's nothing beyond the World's Edge, just mist," Abe added. "Everyone knows that. Nobody's ever made it through that mist."

Nobody? Nick thought. But didn't someone once? someone lonely and cold— But no, he thought with a shiver. That's ridiculous. We've always lived in the Valley, all together. I don't remember a time when we weren't all here.

"Great riddle, Otto," he cried, "even if it doesn't have an answer! Now, how about a song!"

And he led them in almost twenty choruses of "The Bear Went over the Mountain," until Otto's ox turned and gave them such a look, they had to stop.

It was a wonderful day, as he told Willie when he returned.

But that night, Nick dreamed the most terrible dream of all.

This dream was not like the other ones. This time, everything seemed quite normal.

In this dream, he was walking through the underground power tunnels that fueled the village's machinery. His friends were there, arguing about the tunnel's ceiling, and whether it would bear up against the weight of all those daffodils and dolls. Nonsense, said Nick, flowers and toys aren't too heavy.

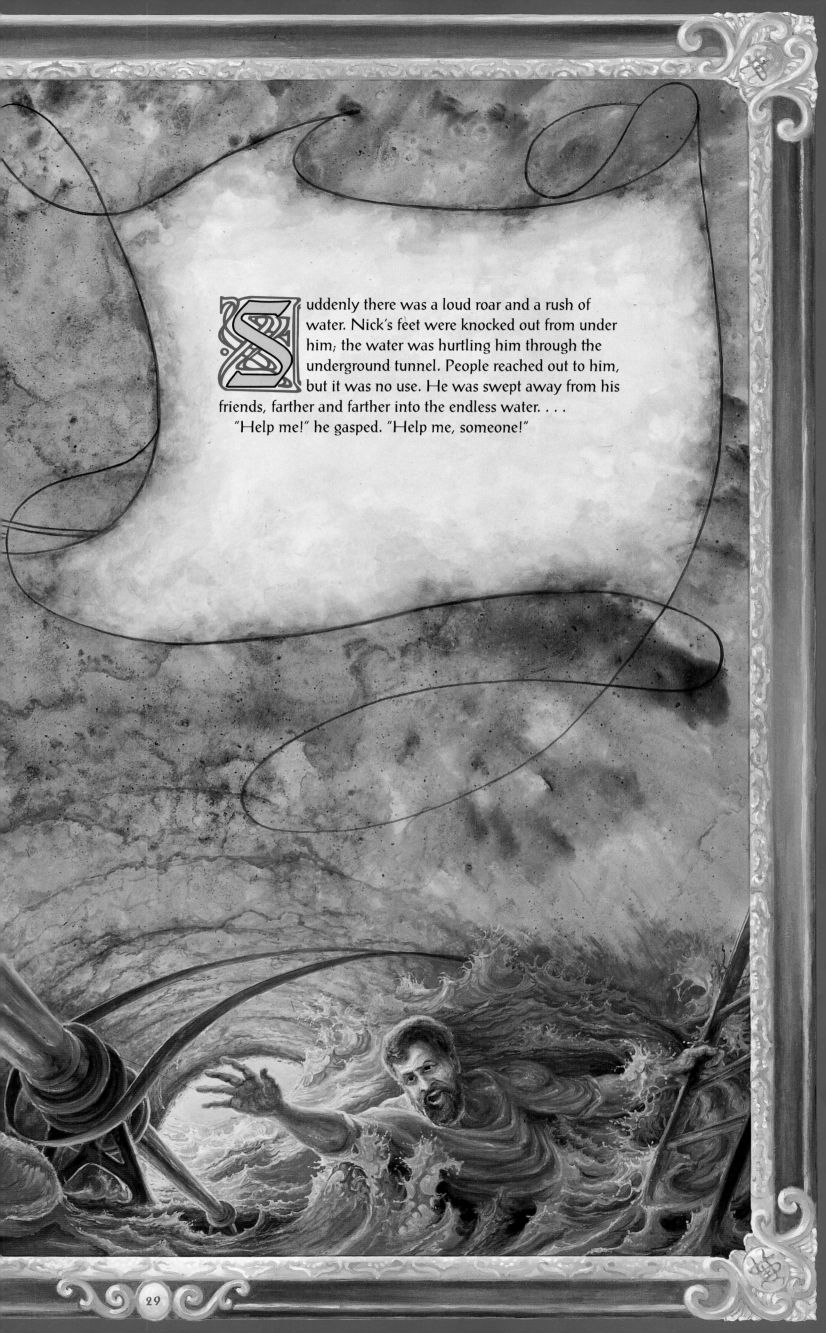

Suddenly there was a loud roar and a rush of water. Nick's feet were knocked out from under him; the water was hurtling him through the underground tunnel. People reached out to him, but it was no use. He was swept away from his friends, farther and farther into the endless water. . . .

"Help me!" he gasped. "Help me, someone!"

ick woke up struggling in his blankets as though they were water. He took deep breaths of the clean night air. He was safe. He was all right now. It was only another dream, after all.

But if that was so, then why could he still hear cries for help? He lit the candle by his bedside. The warm yellow glow filled the room.

And there, on the end of his bed, a little boy sat crying.

"I'm cold," the boy sobbed. "I'm cold and I'm hungry, I'm scared and I'm tired, and I'm all *alone!*"

"Who are you?" Nick exclaimed. "Where did you come from?"

The boy took one look at him and shrieked. "You're a grown-up! You're big and horrible, and you're going to *hurt* me!"

"No, no, I'm not." Nick stumbled out of bed to him. "I won't hurt you. I'm going to wrap you in this nice warm blanket—see? And then I'm going to take you downstairs for some nice warm milk, and you won't be so hungry."

Willie found them in the kitchen.

"A child!" Willie blinked. "Where did you find a child at this time of night?"

Nick shrugged sleepily. "In my dreams, I think. He was on the bed. Where were you?"

"I couldn't sleep. I was up on the roof, looking at the moon. A child! Only imagine! I don't think there's been a child in the Valley Beyond the World's Edge since . . . well, to tell you the truth, I'm not sure *when* I've seen a child here! He looks so thin and hungry. Why don't you give him something to eat, Nick?"

"I did," her husband said helplessly. "So far he's drunk all the milk, eaten all the bread and cheese and half a salami!"

The child had stopped crying. But his eyes were huge in his thin face. "Hungry," he whispered.

Willie dug into the pantry and came up with some preserved cherries and a crock of pickles for him.

"I think I'll call you Wolfie," she said, "because you are just as hungry as a young wolf cub that's been alone in the hills all winter long."

Nick said, "Why not take our little Wolf to the bakery tomorrow? He won't stay hungry *there* for very long."

They put the child to bed in a little room above the waterfall, and the great round moon of Moon Castle shone in his window all night long.

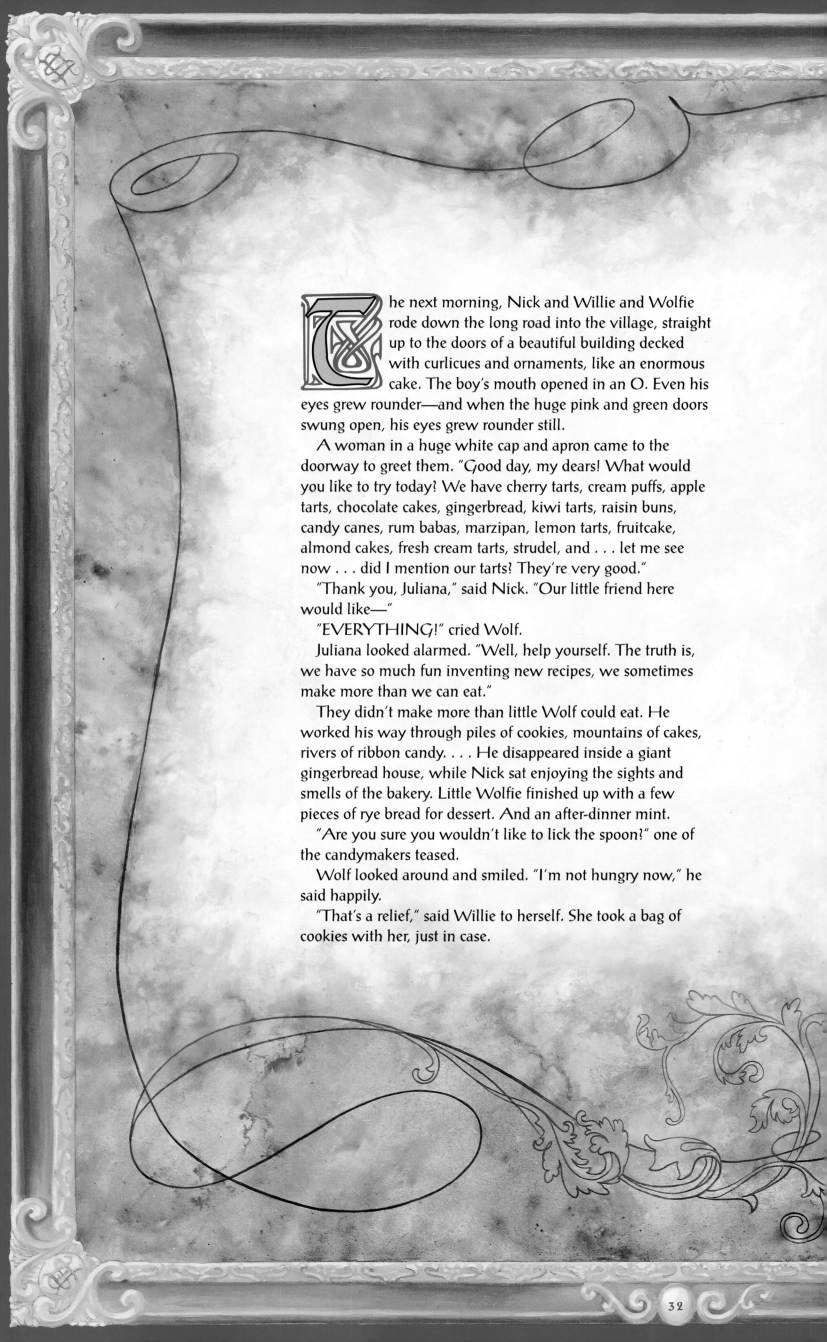

he next morning, Nick and Willie and Wolfie rode down the long road into the village, straight up to the doors of a beautiful building decked with curlicues and ornaments, like an enormous cake. The boy's mouth opened in an O. Even his eyes grew rounder—and when the huge pink and green doors swung open, his eyes grew rounder still.

A woman in a huge white cap and apron came to the doorway to greet them. "Good day, my dears! What would you like to try today! We have cherry tarts, cream puffs, apple tarts, chocolate cakes, gingerbread, kiwi tarts, raisin buns, candy canes, rum babas, marzipan, lemon tarts, fruitcake, almond cakes, fresh cream tarts, strudel, and . . . let me see now . . . did I mention our tarts? They're very good."

"Thank you, Juliana," said Nick. "Our little friend here would like—"

"EVERYTHING!" cried Wolf.

Juliana looked alarmed. "Well, help yourself. The truth is, we have so much fun inventing new recipes, we sometimes make more than we can eat."

They didn't make more than little Wolf could eat. He worked his way through piles of cookies, mountains of cakes, rivers of ribbon candy. . . . He disappeared inside a giant gingerbread house, while Nick sat enjoying the sights and smells of the bakery. Little Wolfie finished up with a few pieces of rye bread for dessert. And an after-dinner mint.

"Are you sure you wouldn't like to lick the spoon?" one of the candymakers teased.

Wolf looked around and smiled. "I'm not hungry now," he said happily.

"That's a relief," said Willie to herself. She took a bag of cookies with her, just in case.

ell!" Nick said as they walke
down the village street
together. "Now that you're
not so hungry—have you eve
visited a woodworkers' shop

Through the carved wooden doors, the
trio entered a world of smells as sweet as
those of the bakery: the smell of wood
being shaved and turned, chipped and
polished under the hands of the craftsmen

The boy ran forward, toward the
scattered toys on the floor. And suddenly
Nick found himself sitting alone in the
middle of them, picking up blocks and
trucks, carved boats and trains, examining
them with as much wonder and delight
as if he'd never seen such things before.

Peter, the tall master carver, laughed. "I
you like them so much, Nick, you might a
well take as many as you want. The truth i
we have so much fun making new ones, w
don't quite know what to do with them all.

Nick stopped, a little confused and
embarrassed. "Thanks. It's not for me, it's
for . . . a friend. Willie—where's Wolfie?
he demanded.

"Why," Willie said, "I thought he was
here. With you. But I don't see him."

"Did someone come in with you?" Pete
asked.

There was a sudden cry from the othe

end of the shop. Willie raced there, in time to see the wooden marionettes dancing in the air above the little stage. The people gazed in wonder. No one held the strings, and yet they danced. She heard a child's laughter.

There was Wolf, standing behind them, his empty hands raised high. And the puppets danced. They danced like fools, like sparrows on a May morning. They danced as if they had never heard of grief or gravity. They danced as if they heard the music of babies laughing.

Then the boy dropped his arms, and the puppets dropped to the stage, lifeless once more, in a broken-jointed tangle of strings.

"Who is this child?" Peter demanded. "Where did he come from?" As Peter ran forward, Wolfie raised his hands over his head once more.

"Don't!" he shrieked. "I was only playing! Don't hurt me, I didn't mean any harm!"

Nick felt his heart crack in sorrow. "He's ours," he told Peter. "Willie's and mine; we found him. The toys are for him."

Wolf looked wildly around him, as though danger could come from anywhere. "I want to go home!" he said frantically to Nick.

"Come," Nick told the boy. "We'll take you home to Moon Castle."

Willie murmured, "No, Nick, you know it's much too long a trip for one day. We'll stop at the inn, the Bell and Stars, the way we always do. He'll be all right there."

His arms piled with toys, Nick whispered to Wolf, "Tomorrow you can play some more."

olf slept that night in a little room in the Bell and Stars, his new toys around him, half a cookie clutched in his fist. Downstairs, Nick and Willie enjoyed the comforts of food and fire, music and friends.

Between the oysters and the plum cake, Willie leaned over to Nick. "And just how," she murmured, "do you suppose Wolf did that little trick with the marionettes?"

Nick shrugged. "I don't know. Isn't it . . . something *all* children can do?"

She looked at him helplessly. "I don't know!"

"Well, we'll find out, I guess. Why don't we take him to the Doll House tomorrow!"

"Nick," his wife asked, "who is he! Where did he come from?"

Nick sighed. "I don't know. Maybe I dreamed him."

Willie hugged him. "Sometimes, Nick, you're a wonderful dreamer."

They fell asleep wrapped in feather quilts. And if Nick dreamed anything at all that night, he did not remember it.

The Doll House of the village was full of people measuring and cutting, snipping and sewing, molding and shaping. Nick, Willie, and Wolf stepped through its tall glass doors into a world of light and laughter, a house made not just for people but for pandas and tigers, brides and princesses.

"Oh, I love dolls!" Willie scooped one up in her arms. "I know it's undignified, but I just can't help myself."

Sitting happily among the stuffed animals, Nick said, "'Undignified?' I don't know what you mean!"

Willie looked down with sudden worry. The child was nowhere in sight. "Oh, no. Where's Wolf?" She wasn't sure she could deal with any dancing toys this morning.

But before anyone could answer, two friends, doll makers, came into the shop, carrying identical dolls in their arms. "You're not going to believe this," Nina said. "We've just designed the exact same doll. See? I feel so silly. What are we going to do with two of them?"

"We're twins!" the dolls squeaked. "Little twin sisters!"

Willie gasped.

Then, laughing, Wolf popped out from behind a panda bigger than himself. "Twins!" he squeaked in the doll voice.

Nora shook herself all over. "That's scary! For a minute there, I thought the dolls were actually talking. Hello, little boy."

"Hello," he answered. "The dolls *are* talking. They say they're lonely."

One of the women in the shop laughed softly. "It's a thought. I sometimes wonder. . . . It's just that, to tell you the truth, we so love bringing new dolls into the world, maybe we don't think enough about where they're going once they're here."

The boy said, "I think you should find them all homes."

Willie said, "That's a lovely thought, Wolfie. Maybe, when you've gotten to know the Valley better, you'll find some people you want to give dolls to."

"I wish you would!" Nina sighed. "Find a nice home for our twins, why don't you! It would be a shame to separate them now."

"Right!" said Nick. He was beginning to get itchy. He wanted to get on to his own very favorite shop.

At the far end of the village, hewn from the granite bluffs above the river, rose the towers of the House of Iron. Inside was all clatter and clang, the hiss of steam and of molten ore poured into sand molds. Willie held Wolf's hand tightly. She didn't want him getting up to anything in *here*, between the liquid fire and turning wheels.

But she need not have worried. Wolf hung back, shy of the noise and clatter. It was Nick who ran forward, exclaiming over the trucks and locomotives, gleaming and perfect and new, the tracks and scenery for making the greatest train sets anyone had ever seen.

The ironworkers clustered around Nick, eager to show him their new work, the improvements to the shapes and forms of burnished metal toys.

Nick held up a new engine. "What do you think, Wolfie! Should we get a new train set for your room up at Moon Castle?"

The boy pointed. "What's that thing!"

"What is it? Why, it's—it's a locomotive. Haven't you ever ridden on a train?" The boy shook his head. "It's big, and noisy, and goes very, very fast—faster than the wind!" The boy grinned. "Would you like to ride in one?" The boy nodded enthusiastically.

"Well," said Nick, "maybe we'll do that! We'll take a trip up the Valley, with boxes of dolls, and make sure everyone has one!" The sad and serious little boy giggled. Nick turned to his Willie. "Well, how about it! What do you say to a train trip up the Valley?"

Willie sighed. She hated trains. "Nasty, smelly things. They go too fast and get cinders all over me. *I'd* rather walk or ride a nice, dependable oxcart. But I can see your heart's set on it. You go and take Wolf, Nick. Have yourselves a lovely time. Just make sure he gets enough F-O-O-D."

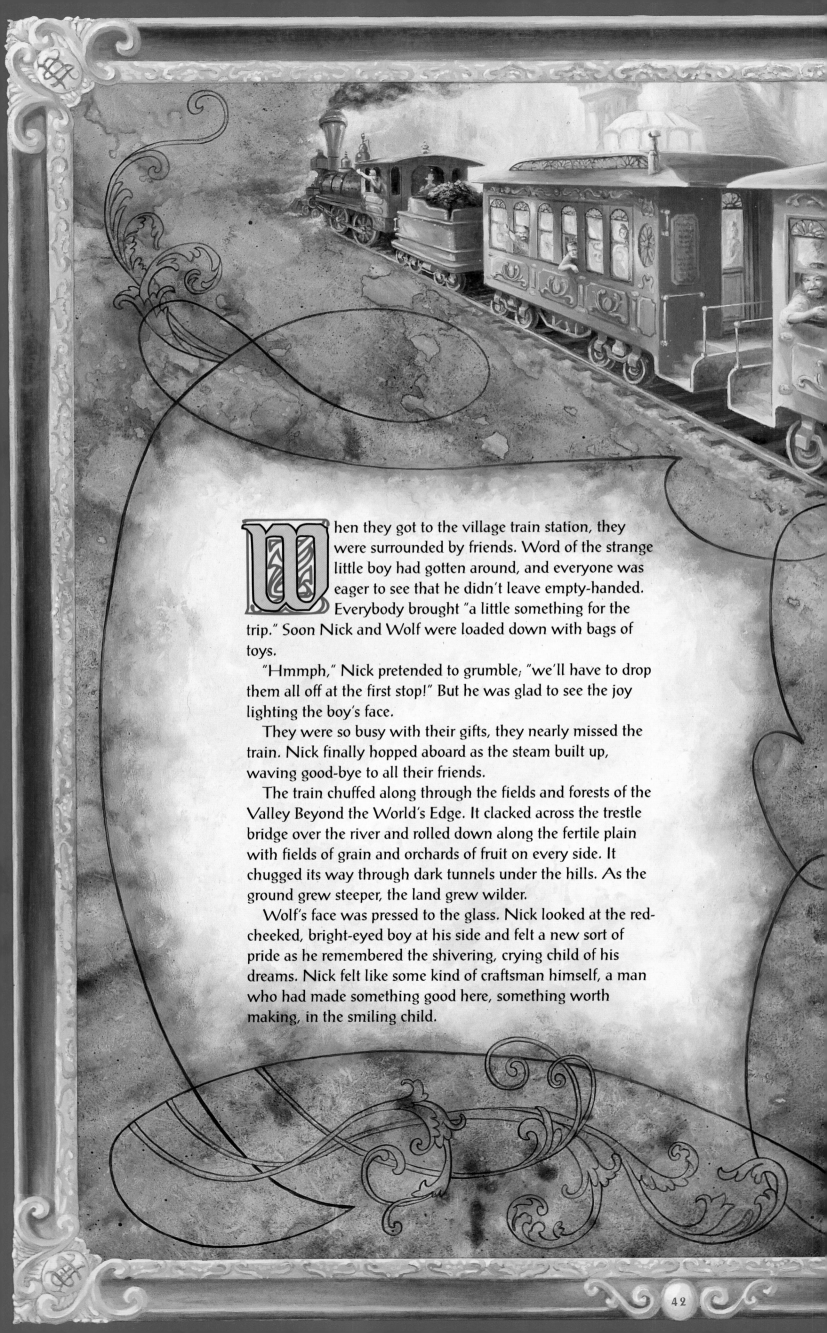

When they got to the village train station, they were surrounded by friends. Word of the strange little boy had gotten around, and everyone was eager to see that he didn't leave empty-handed. Everybody brought "a little something for the trip." Soon Nick and Wolf were loaded down with bags of toys.

"Hmmph," Nick pretended to grumble; "we'll have to drop them all off at the first stop!" But he was glad to see the joy lighting the boy's face.

They were so busy with their gifts, they nearly missed the train. Nick finally hopped aboard as the steam built up, waving good-bye to all their friends.

The train chuffed along through the fields and forests of the Valley Beyond the World's Edge. It clacked across the trestle bridge over the river and rolled down along the fertile plain with fields of grain and orchards of fruit on every side. It chugged its way through dark tunnels under the hills. As the ground grew steeper, the land grew wilder.

Wolf's face was pressed to the glass. Nick looked at the red-cheeked, bright-eyed boy at his side and felt a new sort of pride as he remembered the shivering, crying child of his dreams. Nick felt like some kind of craftsman himself, a man who had made something good here, something worth making, in the smiling child.

It was a long journey up to the Farthest Mountains; they broke it at the farm of Nick's friends Aldo and Sarah. They found Aldo upstairs carving new molds for Sarah's gingerbread.

"Well, they're new and they're not new," Aldo explained. "This is the pattern I've always used for these molds. I'm not like those folks down in the village. I'm not busy, busy, busy, always trying to find something new to improve on the good old ways. I stick to the tried and true. It works, I like it, and I stick to it."

Nick smiled to himself. "And yet I see you've got yourself a different chisel from last time."

Aldo looked up proudly. "Oh, yes! Greg at the foundry fixed this up for me. It's got a hollow edge. Works great,

even better than my old one!"

"Well," said Nick, trying hard not to laugh at his friend, "as long as *you* don't change from the good old ways, I guess it's all right if someone *else* does. . . ."

Aldo grinned. But then his face grew grave. "It's all right for you to joke," he said. "But Nick, I tell you, *someone's* got to remember old ways. With all this making new, new, new, we could sink under the weight of it all."

"Sink?" Nick asked. "What do you mean?"

"Nothing," said Aldo. "That is—well, I've been hearing some strange things lately, from upcountry. Stories about the land, and mysterious trains, and things that really *are* sinking. But you know the kind of stories loggers tell, especially up at the Hazard's Chance camp! It's probably nothing."

Wolf had been gazing quietly at the gingerbread patterns on the wall. Aldo turned: "Here we are talking, when I'll bet you'd like to taste what comes out of these gingerbread molds! I'll go see if Sarah's done baking."

From the rich, spicy scent that filled the farmhouse, they guessed she was just about ready. In the bright, sunny kitchen hung with peppers and herbs and burnished copper pots, Sarah pulled a big cookie from the oven: a gingerbread woman in a lovely old-fashioned costume.

"It's a doll!" cried Wolf.

Sarah said, "It's a doll you can *eat*, my little love." She gave it to the child; and it disappeared in a few bites.

"I'm baking only cookies these days," she confessed to Nick. "Did Aldo tell you! My cakes and breads just haven't been rising lately; they seem so *heavy*, somehow!" She laughed. "Silly, isn't it!"

"I don't think it's silly," the little boy said. "It's hard to keep things from sinking. Maybe I can help. You gave me a doll to eat; I want to give *you* a doll now." And from his sack of toys he pulled a little one from the doll shop for her.

The next morning, Sarah's biscuits rose like clouds.

he train took Nick and Wolf deeper and deeper into the mountains, over gloriously fierce rivers, past waterfalls that tumbled down the sides of deep gorges. But they resisted the urge to get out and sightsee. Nick had a special destination in mind: the Winter Games at Blue Moon Lake.

When at last they arrived, Wolf was so tired he went straight to bed. But Nick hired a sleigh and drove out to see the fun.

Skiers and skaters were everywhere, lit by moon and fire. Nick's old friend Leah took a rest from some fancy figure skating to plop herself down in the sleigh next to him.

"Well, Nick," she teased, "are you going to play ice hockey this year!" She knew skating was not the big man's strongest point! Without giving him a chance to reply, she went on, "Actually, we may have to cancel the game."

"Well, if you want me to play *that* badly—"

Leah shook her head. "That's not it. It's the lake—there's something wrong with it. It seems to be getting smaller. Some of the people think it might be sinking."

"Sinking," Nick said softly. "Too heavy!"

"No one knows why. It doesn't make sense, a lake sinking into the earth. But then, a lot of things these days don't. Take the ski lift. The pulleys and levers keep slipping, as if something were pulling them down. I'm always readjusting them. It's as if—"

"Hey, Leah!" Sam called. "I've made some new skates for you—let's see if we can't get an extra spin on those figure eights!"

"Gotta go!" Leah darted away.

Nick sat for a long time, thinking about heaviness, things sinking, the cold and darkness of his dreams. He wished he could talk to Willie. But Moon Castle was far away. He hated to take Wolf away from the games, but he needed to investigate further.

And so the train and several pack mules took Nick and Wolf and their sack of toys up to the High Plateau, to visit the Ramirez cousins. They all lived together in a white house with a red tile roof, high up where it was always sunny. There, lemons were always fresh for lemonade, and you could pick oranges right off the trees.

The Ramirez cousins made them welcome, and Wolf handed out his toys to them. At the huge feast they made in the shady courtyard, Nick looked for signs of trouble. But nothing was sinking, no one complained of heaviness. In fact, hanging high up on a big tree in the middle of the courtyard was a colorful peacock doll.

"What's that for?" Wolf asked.

"It's a game we play," said Marta Ramirez. "You have to try to hit it with a stick."

"That shouldn't be hard!" Nick said.

Juana Ramirez laughed. "Go ahead, Nick, try it! It's not as easy as you think . . . because first we have to *blindfold* you!" And they did. He couldn't see a thing. "And then . . . we have to *turn you around*!" And they did. They turned him around until he was so dizzy he hardly knew up from down. "All right— now hit the peacock with the stick!"

Well, Nick tried and tried, but all he did was make the doll rock a little in the breeze from his stick. He tore the blindfold off, laughing. "I don't see why we're trying to hit the poor thing in the first place. We might break it!"

The Ramirez cousins shrieked with laughter. "You're supposed to break our piñata! There's candy inside!"

"Well!" said Nick. "Why didn't you say so! Here, Wolfie, you have a try. You like candy!"

"Come on!" they shouted. "Give it a good one!" Privately, Nick thought they had not turned the child around nearly so hard as they had himself. Once, twice, the stick connected gently, and on the third try Wolf struck with a resounding *crack*. Nick caught his breath as the piñata split.

No candy fell from the open belly of the peacock, but flowers, flowers of every season: the spring violet, the autumn goldenrod, the larkspur and marigold. They fell slowly, like flowers in a dream . . . and last of all trailed a long ribbon.

Nobody moved. They all stood and stared.

Finally, Nick picked up the ribbon. The strange flowers melted away as his hand brushed them, like flowers of snow.

On the ribbon were written these words:

What was lost is found
Where rolling rooms are still.
At its edge the world is round.
Now riddle if you will:

NO HANDS CAN MAKE ME.
TWO HANDS CAN SHAPE ME.
ALL HANDS CAN TAKE ME.

"It's the riddle!" Juana Ramirez gasped. "The old Lost Riddle. *No hands can make me* . . . But what are the rolling rooms! And how did it get into our piñata!"

But nobody knew.

"It must be a new clue," said Diego Ramirez, "a way to solve the riddle. But what's the edge of the world?"

Old Alonzo Ramirez spoke up. "The Edge of the World is in the Northern Mountains."

"I thought the Edge of the World was just a legend."

"No," said Alonzo. "It is real. The Edge of the World is a huge mist. No one knows what lies on the other side—if there *is* another side. My brother Sancho tried to find out once. He walked into that mist . . . and he never came back."

Nick was silent, listening, thinking. Once, twice, the Lost Riddle had come to him: on the oxcart, carved into the very walls of his home. This third time, he knew that whatever it meant, whatever he feared, must be faced. This talk of the Edge of the World chilled him in ways he couldn't understand. And that, too, must be faced now.

"I've heard," Nick told his friends, "that to solve the riddle will be to save the Valley. But I didn't know anything was *wrong* with the Valley—not until I made this trip. I had some dreams, but I didn't pay attention to them the way I should have. On this trip I've heard strange things, and seen them, too. . . . I'll go, my friends, and I'll solve the riddle—even if it means going to the World's Edge."

"Me, too!" Wolf piped up.

Nick started to say it was too dangerous —but then he changed his mind. "Yes. After all, it was you who found the riddle." And he thought privately, *Otto said someone would come from beyond the World's Edge to solve it. Maybe my poor little Wolf is the one.*

In the Northern Mountains, Alonzo had said, but exactly where to find the Edge of the World, the old man couldn't tell. For legends and tall tales, Nick knew, no one could beat the deep forest loggers. So he and Wolf rode the train as far as the forest's edge, and took a sleigh out to the loggers' camp at Hazard's Chance, and out to the new stands of timber where axemen and sawyers were busy at their work. They watched in awe as one huge tree fell with slow, steady majesty, like a king bowing to the will of his people, meeting the ground with a sound of thunder.

Then an echoing groan rose up from the foresters. For the tree had begun to sink into the earth, deeper than its weight could account for, as if some force were dragging it down. The men rushed in with ropes and wedges, but it was no good. Nick stared in wonder. It was the sinking, the weight on the land. Like Sarah's cakes, like Blue Moon Lake, like Nick's own bad dreams.

"Wait!" Wolf's voice rang out, high and thin in the winter air. And somehow Nick found himself with his hands in the bag of toys they had carried all this way, pulling out the wooden trucks and puppets, soldiers and sailboats the people in the village had made from the lumber of these very forests.

The stunned leadman took a little truck. A slow smile spread across his face. "Look at that." His large, rough finger ran along the grain of the carved wood, spinning the wheel. "Something from one of our own trees. A nice new truck! Hey, fellas! Come see what they made from our trees this year!"

The other foresters came running. They handled the wooden toys with delight. "All right," the leadman said finally. "Let's get back to work on this—" He stopped with his mouth open wide.

The tree was no longer sinking. It lay easy on the snow, like any fallen tree.

The loggers began bucking the great fir tree for its long journey out of the woods. But all of them carried a wooden toy with them, tucking the toys into their jackets as if they were good luck.

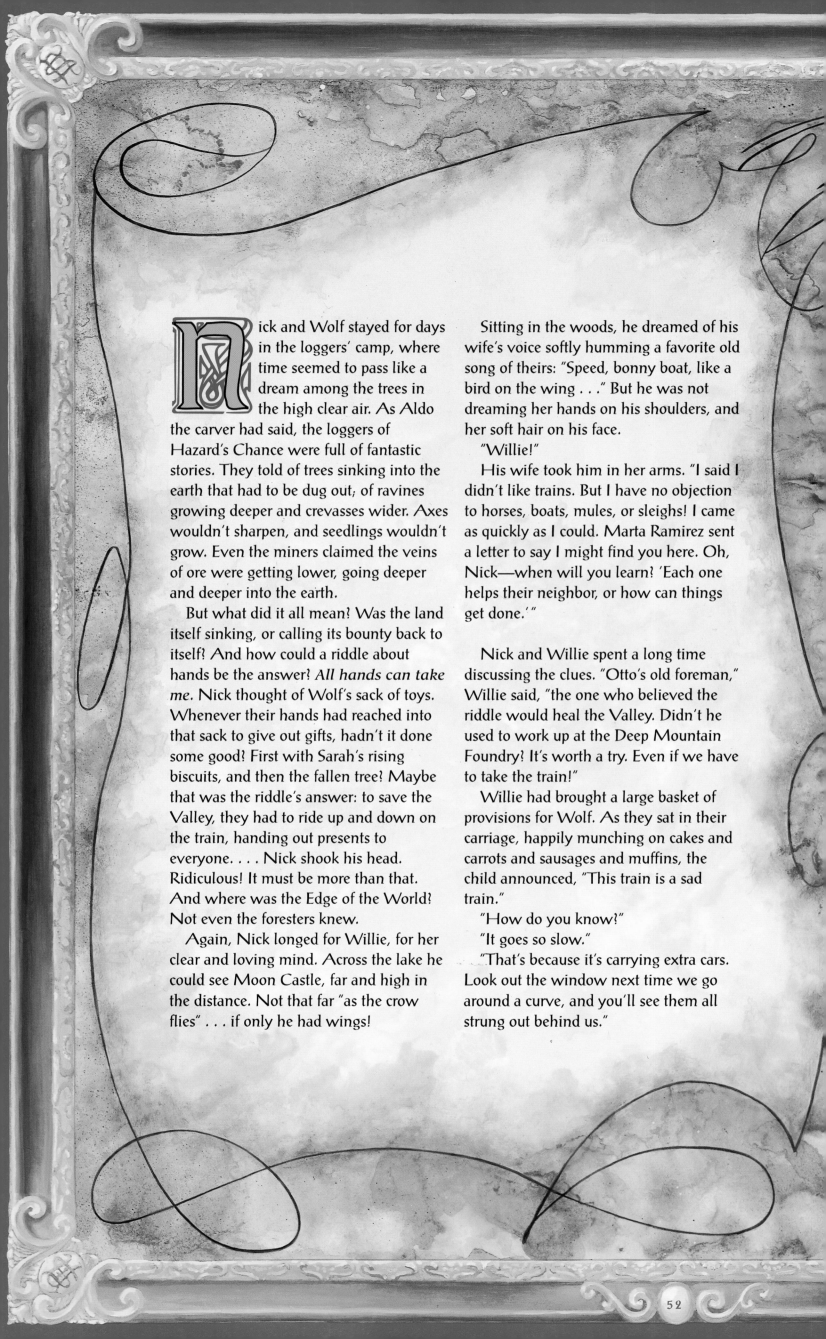

ick and Wolf stayed for days in the loggers' camp, where time seemed to pass like a dream among the trees in the high clear air. As Aldo the carver had said, the loggers of Hazard's Chance were full of fantastic stories. They told of trees sinking into the earth that had to be dug out; of ravines growing deeper and crevasses wider. Axes wouldn't sharpen, and seedlings wouldn't grow. Even the miners claimed the veins of ore were getting lower, going deeper and deeper into the earth.

But what did it all mean? Was the land itself sinking, or calling its bounty back to itself? And how could a riddle about hands be the answer? *All hands can take me.* Nick thought of Wolf's sack of toys. Whenever their hands had reached into that sack to give out gifts, hadn't it done some good? First with Sarah's rising biscuits, and then the fallen tree! Maybe that was the riddle's answer: to save the Valley, they had to ride up and down on the train, handing out presents to everyone. . . . Nick shook his head. Ridiculous! It must be more than that. And where was the Edge of the World? Not even the foresters knew.

Again, Nick longed for Willie, for her clear and loving mind. Across the lake he could see Moon Castle, far and high in the distance. Not that far "as the crow flies" . . . if only he had wings!

Sitting in the woods, he dreamed of his wife's voice softly humming a favorite old song of theirs: "Speed, bonny boat, like a bird on the wing . . ." But he was not dreaming her hands on his shoulders, and her soft hair on his face.

"Willie!"

His wife took him in her arms. "I said I didn't like trains. But I have no objection to horses, boats, mules, or sleighs! I came as quickly as I could. Marta Ramirez sent a letter to say I might find you here. Oh, Nick—when will you learn? 'Each one helps their neighbor, or how can things get done.' "

Nick and Willie spent a long time discussing the clues. "Otto's old foreman," Willie said, "the one who believed the riddle would heal the Valley. Didn't he used to work up at the Deep Mountain Foundry? It's worth a try. Even if we have to take the train!"

Willie had brought a large basket of provisions for Wolf. As they sat in their carriage, happily munching on cakes and carrots and sausages and muffins, the child announced, "This train is a sad train."

"How do you know?"

"It goes so slow."

"That's because it's carrying extra cars. Look out the window next time we go around a curve, and you'll see them all strung out behind us."

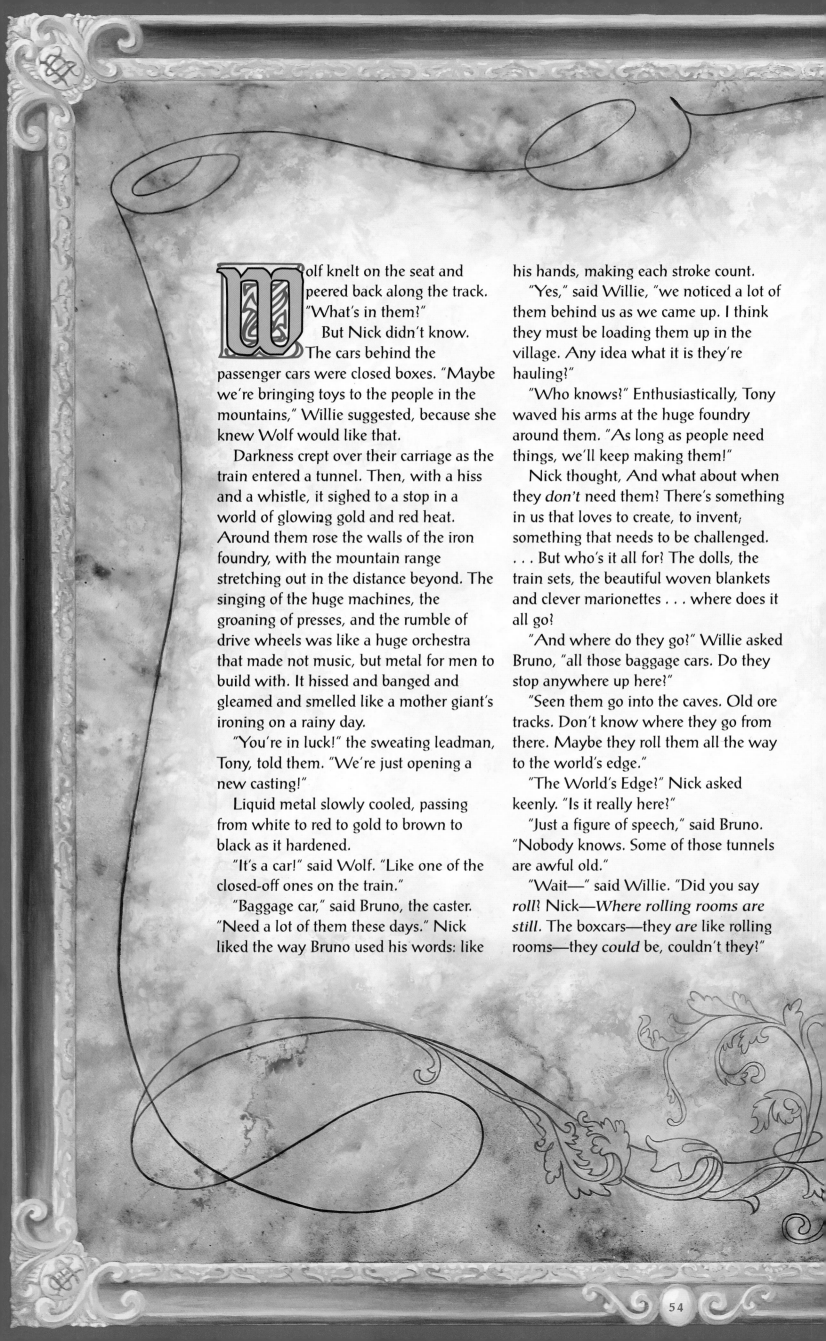

olf knelt on the seat and peered back along the track. "What's in them?"

But Nick didn't know. The cars behind the passenger cars were closed boxes. "Maybe we're bringing toys to the people in the mountains," Willie suggested, because she knew Wolf would like that.

Darkness crept over their carriage as the train entered a tunnel. Then, with a hiss and a whistle, it sighed to a stop in a world of glowing gold and red heat. Around them rose the walls of the iron foundry, with the mountain range stretching out in the distance beyond. The singing of the huge machines, the groaning of presses, and the rumble of drive wheels was like a huge orchestra that made not music, but metal for men to build with. It hissed and banged and gleamed and smelled like a mother giant's ironing on a rainy day.

"You're in luck!" the sweating leadman, Tony, told them. "We're just opening a new casting!"

Liquid metal slowly cooled, passing from white to red to gold to brown to black as it hardened.

"It's a car!" said Wolf. "Like one of the closed-off ones on the train."

"Baggage car," said Bruno, the caster. "Need a lot of them these days." Nick liked the way Bruno used his words: like his hands, making each stroke count.

"Yes," said Willie, "we noticed a lot of them behind us as we came up. I think they must be loading them up in the village. Any idea what it is they're hauling?"

"Who knows!" Enthusiastically, Tony waved his arms at the huge foundry around them. "As long as people need things, we'll keep making them!"

Nick thought, And what about when they *don't* need them? There's something in us that loves to create, to invent; something that needs to be challenged. . . . But who's it all for? The dolls, the train sets, the beautiful woven blankets and clever marionettes . . . where does it all go?

"And where do they go?" Willie asked Bruno, "all those baggage cars. Do they stop anywhere up here?"

"Seen them go into the caves. Old ore tracks. Don't know where they go from there. Maybe they roll them all the way to the world's edge."

"The World's Edge?" Nick asked keenly. "Is it really here?"

"Just a figure of speech," said Bruno. "Nobody knows. Some of those tunnels are awful old."

"Wait—" said Willie. "Did you say *roll*? Nick—*Where rolling rooms are still.* The boxcars—they *are* like rolling rooms—they *could* be, couldn't they?"

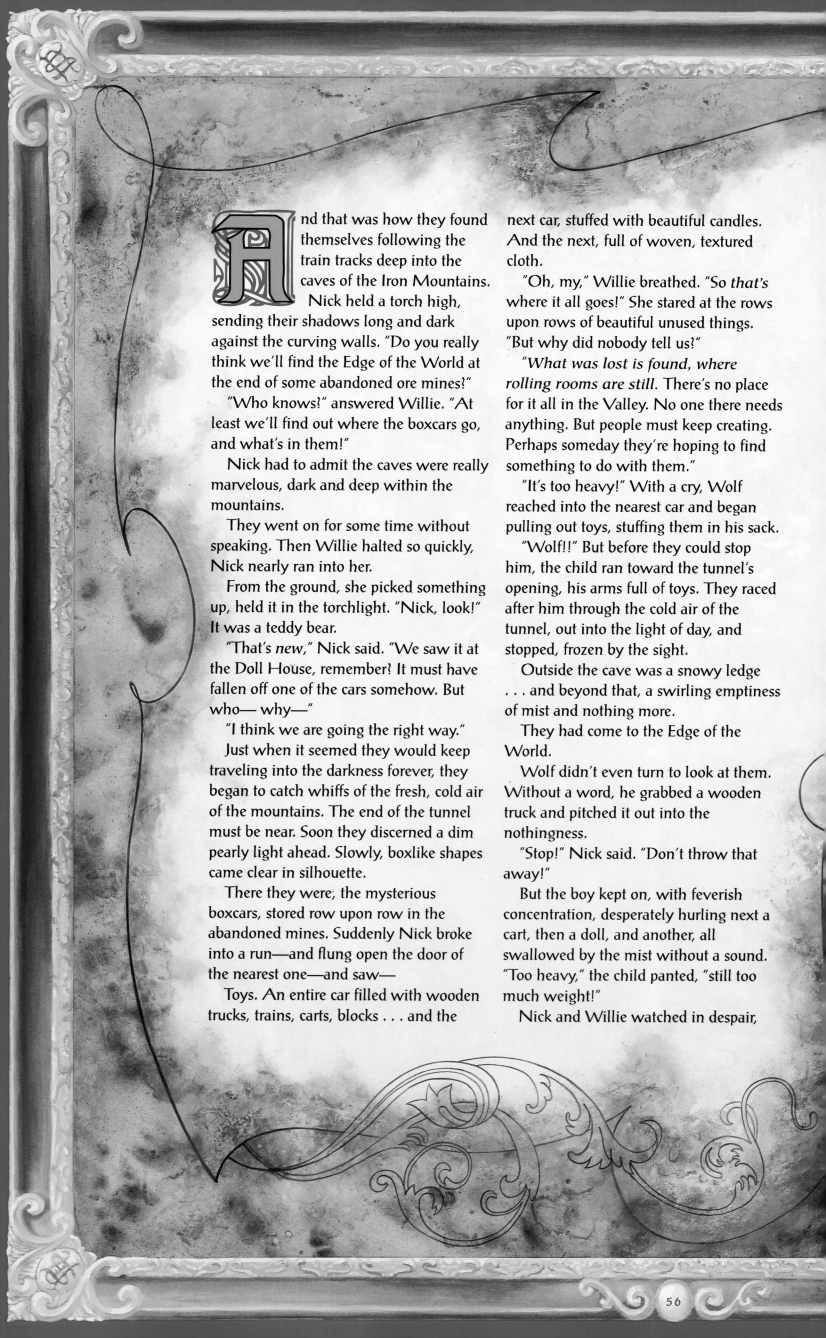

And that was how they found themselves following the train tracks deep into the caves of the Iron Mountains. Nick held a torch high, sending their shadows long and dark against the curving walls. "Do you really think we'll find the Edge of the World at the end of some abandoned ore mines?"

"Who knows?" answered Willie. "At least we'll find out where the boxcars go, and what's in them!"

Nick had to admit the caves were really marvelous, dark and deep within the mountains.

They went on for some time without speaking. Then Willie halted so quickly, Nick nearly ran into her.

From the ground, she picked something up, held it in the torchlight. "Nick, look!" It was a teddy bear.

"That's *new*," Nick said. "We saw it at the Doll House, remember? It must have fallen off one of the cars somehow. But who— why—"

"I think we are going the right way."

Just when it seemed they would keep traveling into the darkness forever, they began to catch whiffs of the fresh, cold air of the mountains. The end of the tunnel must be near. Soon they discerned a dim pearly light ahead. Slowly, boxlike shapes came clear in silhouette.

There they were; the mysterious boxcars, stored row upon row in the abandoned mines. Suddenly Nick broke into a run—and flung open the door of the nearest one—and saw—

Toys. An entire car filled with wooden trucks, trains, carts, blocks . . . and the next car, stuffed with beautiful candles. And the next, full of woven, textured cloth.

"Oh, my," Willie breathed. "So *that's* where it all goes!" She stared at the rows upon rows of beautiful unused things. "But why did nobody tell us?"

"*What was lost is found, where rolling rooms are still.* There's no place for it all in the Valley. No one there needs anything. But people must keep creating. Perhaps someday they're hoping to find something to do with them."

"It's too heavy!" With a cry, Wolf reached into the nearest car and began pulling out toys, stuffing them in his sack.

"Wolf!!" But before they could stop him, the child ran toward the tunnel's opening, his arms full of toys. They raced after him through the cold air of the tunnel, out into the light of day, and stopped, frozen by the sight.

Outside the cave was a snowy ledge . . . and beyond that, a swirling emptiness of mist and nothing more.

They had come to the Edge of the World.

Wolf didn't even turn to look at them. Without a word, he grabbed a wooden truck and pitched it out into the nothingness.

"Stop!" Nick said. "Don't throw that away!"

But the boy kept on, with feverish concentration, desperately hurling next a cart, then a doll, and another, all swallowed by the mist without a sound. "Too heavy," the child panted, "still too much weight!"

Nick and Willie watched in despair,

not knowing how to help. This fierce, purposeful little creature was beyond them.

Willie muttered, "Wait a minute. I think I've got an apple, maybe that will calm him down."

Nick handed him the apple. "Here. Now be a good boy and stop throwing things." But Wolf only hurled another doll into the mist.

"I said, STOP!" Nick shouted, and gripped him, hard.

The boy turned blazing eyes on him. "You forgot. You forgot everything! I'm just getting rid of the heaviness, and you can't even see it!" He began shoving toys into his sack. "You'll never understand!"

Before they could stop him, the child leaped forward.

"No—wait!"

But it was too late. Nick held out his empty hands as Wolf disappeared over the Edge of the World.

or a moment Nick hesitated, remembering the Ramirez brother who had stepped off the World's Edge and never returned. But only for a moment. Then he plunged into the mist after the child.

"Wolf!" he shouted. The mist was thick and white as cotton. "Wolf, come back!"

The mist began to thin. Ahead of him, a small, dark-haired boy stood alone on a hillside above a little village. Memory's chilly fingers gripped Nick and would not let him go.

"I know this place," Nick said. "I've been here before." He felt cold and hungry and afraid. "But I don't want to remember! It was terrible!"

"It's all right," the boy said. "Here." He took the apple, and cut it in half. "I've got a special present, just for you. The Apple Star—remember?"

Nick saw: the two halves of the apple split to show a cross-section, a five-pointed star. Nick saw, and he remembered.

As Nick reached out his hand to take it, he felt himself changing, as though layer after layer of himself were being peeled away, exposed to air. He saw the child's hands, and they were his own hands. His little hands on a cold Christmas morning, holding an apple that was a star, the only gift his poor mother could give him before she went on a long journey where even he could not follow.

"I remember," Nick said to the child he had been. "When she was gone, I was all alone. If I hadn't found my way to the Valley, I think I would have died, too. I never wanted to come back here! And so I forgot it all—even the Apple Star! Thank you for giving that back to me."

He looked at the sack of toys the boy carried. "I should not have forgotten." Picking up the sack, Nick tried to smile. "But now that I'm here, at least I can bring them some presents from the Valley—"

"No." The boy took the sack from him. "You still don't understand. You don't belong here anymore. You can't stay here. You already grew up, in the Valley. I have to stay and grow up here. People will need me here, the way they need you back there."

Nick looked at the boy sadly. "Oh, Wolfie. Will I ever see you again?"

The boy smiled. "Every day. I'll always be there if you remember me. Don't you know me yet? My name is Nicholas."

The mist closed around him, and Nick was alone.

It was cold in the mist, and so silent he could not hear his own breathing. He started walking, but he was wrapped in timeless emptiness, lost between the Valley and the World's Edge. Was he a grown man, Nick wondered, or a child still lost and alone on a cold, cold night?

Then it seemed to him that he grew warmer, and somehow less alone. And a voice in his head said, "Keep going. Keep walking."

It was a voice full of kindness, a voice that lived in warmth and light. Then warm, furry bodies were on either side of him, lending him their strength. Then, ahead of him, a light began to glow. And there stood Willie, her arms open wide.

As Nick and Willie embraced at the World's Edge, all around them graceful animals pranced and wheeled. Handsome as deer, fluid as rain, they coursed around the two people as Nick poured out to Willie the truth of Wolf and of the world on the other side of the mist. "I was so afraid"—Nick hugged her tight—"afraid I would never find my way back to you!"

"Did we not tell you once," the lovely creatures said, "that this is your home?"

"It was you!" Nick said. "You are the ones who led me here when I was a cold and lonely boy!"

"We are the Raindeer," they told him, "the Guardians of the Valley. For longer than you know, we have kept this place a haven, where the great crafters and artisans, farmers and workers could follow their skills in peace. But it could not continue thus forever. The land grows weary of its gifts going nowhere. It sinks under the weight of its own bounty. And so we brought you here."

"But how can I help? If only I could release the land from its heaviness—but I haven't yet solved the riddle!"

The Raindeer laughed among themselves. "Never mind," they told him. "You can still do some good to the Valley and to that World you come from."

Nick said, "If only there were some way of getting the Valley's gifts to the people in the World who need them. If I could just do it myself—"

The Raindeers' laughter snuggled Nick and Willie like blankets. And Nick understood.

"That's it, isn't it?" he cried. "I'm the only one who can go through the mist and back again, from the Valley to the World. That's why you brought me. Wolf said I didn't belong there anymore—but that doesn't mean I can't go back and forth!"

"Ah!" the Raindeer said. "Now you understand!"

Willie said, "But why didn't you tell Nick all this when you first brought him here?"

One floated up into the sky and drifted down beside them. "He wasn't ready. He had too much to forget. And then he had too much to remember.

"Jump on our backs!" the Raindeer said. "Come, Nick and Willie, and we will show you how easy it is to sail over field and forest, river and mountain!"

As they passed overhead, people looked up and pointed with wonder and amazement. The Raindeer set Nick down in a little valley sprinkled with trees, where a cozy house nestled against the hill. Bruce, the holly farmer, just stood leaning on his axe. "Nick," he said, "you've done some weird things in your time, but this one beats all!"

But when Nick told Bruce of his plans, the holly farmer was ecstatic. "You mean all our toys are going somewhere where people really need them? Great! How soon do we start packing?"

Nick thought of the Apple Star, his mother's Christmas gift. "I think," he said, "we can wait until December. There are so many people in the World who need a little extra kindness at Christmas."

"I don't know," Bruce grumbled, "Christmas is an awfully long way away. . . ."

Willie, who had finally landed, said, "And how will we know which things to send to the World? Everyone will want to send their very best—how will we be able to pick from among them all?"

Nick snapped his fingers. "I know! A fair. This spring, as soon as the snow melts, we'll have a huge festival, a Springfest, down in the village. Everyone in the Valley can come and show off their very best work. That way we can all

admire what everyone's up to, learn from each other, and have a really great time planning our gifts for the World at Christmas!"

Willie kissed him. "What a wonderful man you are! Let's hurry up and tell everyone. The Raindeer—"

But the Raindeer had gone. "Oh, they'll be back," said Nick confidently. "They'll know when we need them."

"But we need them *now!*" Willie protested. "How are we going to get home to Moon Castle or tell all our friends about the Springfest?"

Bruce smiled. "Hmm," he said. "I think I can help you out with that one."

And that is how Nick and Willie found themselves once more high above the ground, this time carried in the hot-air balloons the foresters used to harvest old timber from new growth!

As they passed over farm and field, the balloons dipped so they could shout out the good news: a Springfest, and Christmas gifts for the World!

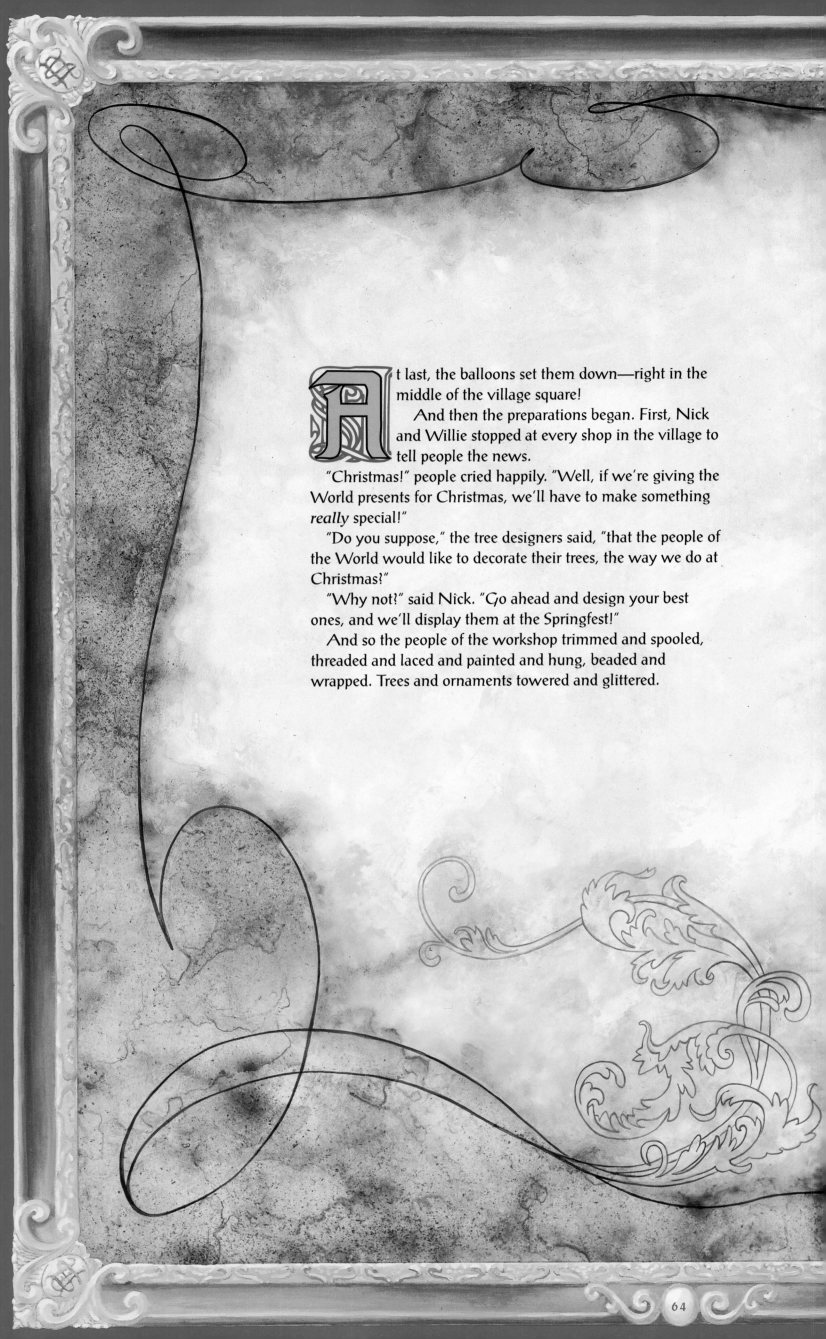

At last, the balloons set them down—right in the middle of the village square!

And then the preparations began. First, Nick and Willie stopped at every shop in the village to tell people the news.

"Christmas!" people cried happily. "Well, if we're giving the World presents for Christmas, we'll have to make something *really* special!"

"Do you suppose," the tree designers said, "that the people of the World would like to decorate their trees, the way we do at Christmas!"

"Why not!" said Nick. "Go ahead and design your best ones, and we'll display them at the Springfest!"

And so the people of the workshop trimmed and spooled, threaded and laced and painted and hung, beaded and wrapped. Trees and ornaments towered and glittered.

Do you suppose," the electricians said, "that the people of the World would like to hang their trees with lights, the way we do at Christmas!"

"It's a thought," Nick said diplomatically, adding under his breath, "if you can really get that danged *electricity* to work!"

So the light makers carefully blew their bulbs of many-colored glass and did strange things with wires and amps and volts that no one else could understand, and the shop blazed with the light of the glorious trees.

Willie muttered, "This is getting out of hand. At this rate, it's going to be Christmas in this village all year round!"

"And what's wrong with that!" Nick laughed. "You know —I *like* the idea!" And Willie had to admit that she did, too.

"Well," she said, "now that we've got the trees taken care of, hadn't we better make sure there's something nice to put under them!"

A bsolutely!" Nick said, "What about toy soldiers? I'll go see how they're doing."

The scene in the studio was sheer chaos. Someone there had heard about the Springfest and decided that all their old work wasn't good enough; they had to try for even better toys. This seemed to involve one of them, Sebastian, creating a new uniform and a new pose for the soldiers, which seemed to involve him getting up on a table to model them, while all the other artisans hastily did their best to capture the moment.

The moment was rapidly disintegrating, as every single artist called out a different need to him:

"Look happier!"

"Look sterner!"

"Clench your fist!"

"Straighten your hat!"

"A little more to the left!"

"A bit more to the right!"

"DON'T MOVE!"

Before Sebastian could fly into a million pieces, "Perfect!" cried Nick. "I know the new soldiers will be the hit of the Springfest! Can't wait to see you there."

And he hurried on down the street to the tailor shop, only to discover his first real surprise—

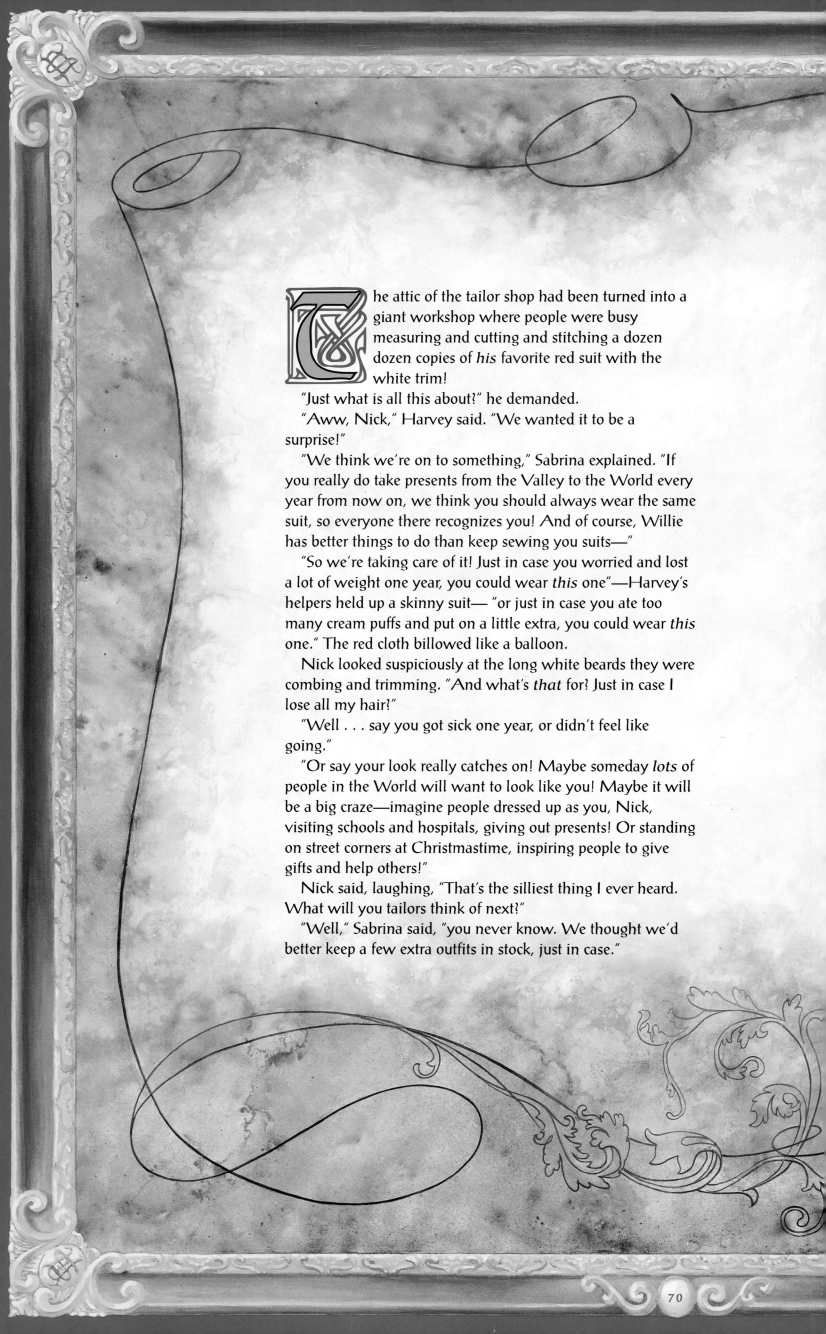

The attic of the tailor shop had been turned into a giant workshop where people were busy measuring and cutting and stitching a dozen dozen copies of *his* favorite red suit with the white trim!

"Just what is all this about?" he demanded.

"Aww, Nick," Harvey said. "We wanted it to be a surprise!"

"We think we're on to something," Sabrina explained. "If you really do take presents from the Valley to the World every year from now on, we think you should always wear the same suit, so everyone there recognizes you! And of course, Willie has better things to do than keep sewing you suits—"

"So we're taking care of it! Just in case you worried and lost a lot of weight one year, you could wear *this* one"—Harvey's helpers held up a skinny suit— "or just in case you ate too many cream puffs and put on a little extra, you could wear *this* one." The red cloth billowed like a balloon.

Nick looked suspiciously at the long white beards they were combing and trimming. "And what's *that* for? Just in case I lose all my hair?"

"Well . . . say you got sick one year, or didn't feel like going."

"Or say your look really catches on! Maybe someday *lots* of people in the World will want to look like you! Maybe it will be a big craze—imagine people dressed up as you, Nick, visiting schools and hospitals, giving out presents! Or standing on street corners at Christmastime, inspiring people to give gifts and help others!"

Nick said, laughing, "That's the silliest thing I ever heard. What will you tailors think of next?"

"Well," Sabrina said, "you never know. We thought we'd better keep a few extra outfits in stock, just in case."

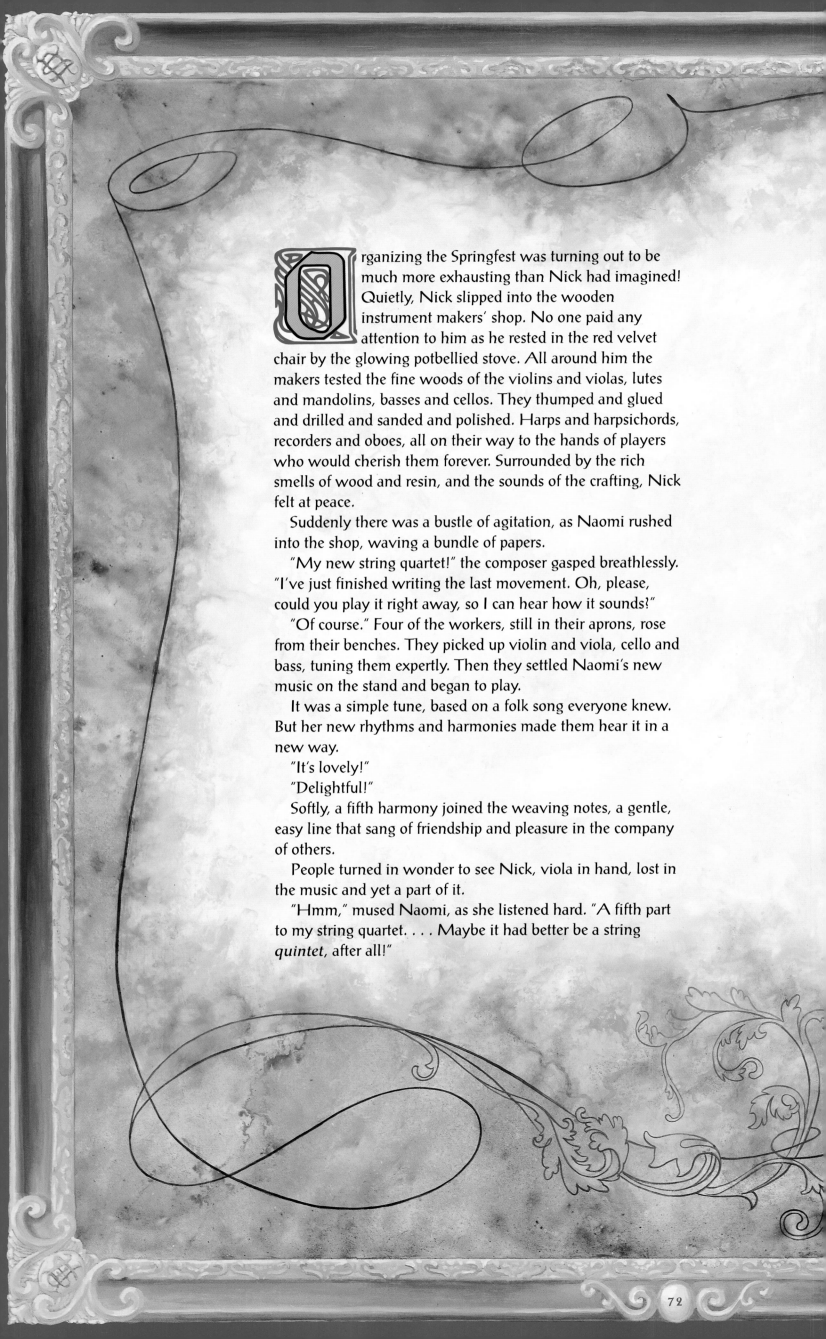

rganizing the Springfest was turning out to be much more exhausting than Nick had imagined! Quietly, Nick slipped into the wooden instrument makers' shop. No one paid any attention to him as he rested in the red velvet chair by the glowing potbellied stove. All around him the makers tested the fine woods of the violins and violas, lutes and mandolins, basses and cellos. They thumped and glued and drilled and sanded and polished. Harps and harpsichords, recorders and oboes, all on their way to the hands of players who would cherish them forever. Surrounded by the rich smells of wood and resin, and the sounds of the crafting, Nick felt at peace.

Suddenly there was a bustle of agitation, as Naomi rushed into the shop, waving a bundle of papers.

"My new string quartet!" the composer gasped breathlessly. "I've just finished writing the last movement. Oh, please, could you play it right away, so I can hear how it sounds?"

"Of course." Four of the workers, still in their aprons, rose from their benches. They picked up violin and viola, cello and bass, tuning them expertly. Then they settled Naomi's new music on the stand and began to play.

It was a simple tune, based on a folk song everyone knew. But her new rhythms and harmonies made them hear it in a new way.

"It's lovely!"

"Delightful!"

Softly, a fifth harmony joined the weaving notes, a gentle, easy line that sang of friendship and pleasure in the company of others.

People turned in wonder to see Nick, viola in hand, lost in the music and yet a part of it.

"Hmm," mused Naomi, as she listened hard. "A fifth part to my string quartet. . . . Maybe it had better be a string *quintet*, after all!"

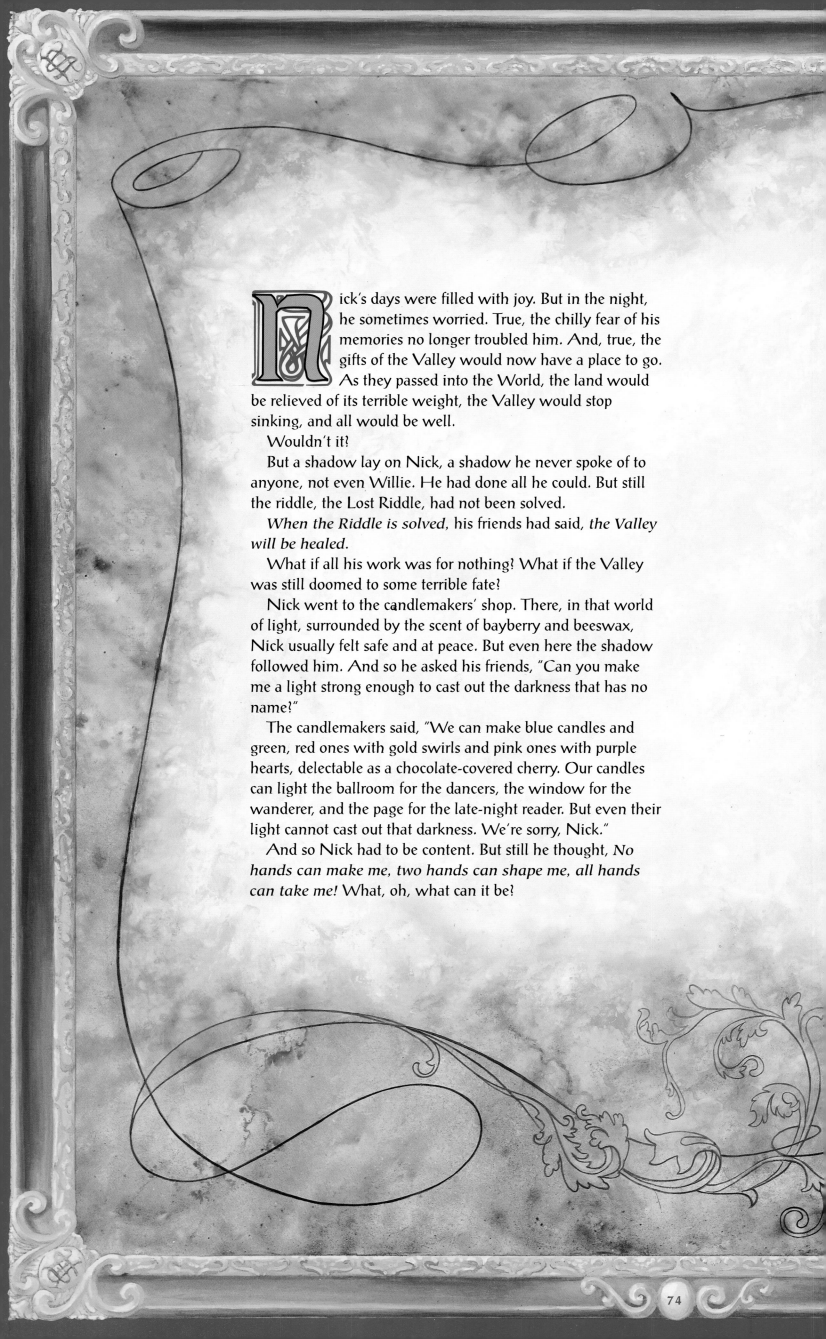

ick's days were filled with joy. But in the night, he sometimes worried. True, the chilly fear of his memories no longer troubled him. And, true, the gifts of the Valley would now have a place to go. As they passed into the World, the land would be relieved of its terrible weight, the Valley would stop sinking, and all would be well.

Wouldn't it?

But a shadow lay on Nick, a shadow he never spoke of to anyone, not even Willie. He had done all he could. But still the riddle, the Lost Riddle, had not been solved.

When the Riddle is solved, his friends had said, *the Valley will be healed.*

What if all his work was for nothing! What if the Valley was still doomed to some terrible fate?

Nick went to the candlemakers' shop. There, in that world of light, surrounded by the scent of bayberry and beeswax, Nick usually felt safe and at peace. But even here the shadow followed him. And so he asked his friends, "Can you make me a light strong enough to cast out the darkness that has no name?"

The candlemakers said, "We can make blue candles and green, red ones with gold swirls and pink ones with purple hearts, delectable as a chocolate-covered cherry. Our candles can light the ballroom for the dancers, the window for the wanderer, and the page for the late-night reader. But even their light cannot cast out that darkness. We're sorry, Nick."

And so Nick had to be content. But still he thought, *No hands can make me, two hands can shape me, all hands can take me!* What, oh, what can it be?

On the morning of the Springfest, Nick and Willie put on their best clothes and hurried to the village square.

For days, people had been pouring in from all over the Valley, in carts and on muleback, on special trains from the mountains and by boat downriver, bringing their very best work to show, hoping it would be selected as the Valley's gift to the World this year.

Every room in the village was full. Now every inch of the square was crammed with booths and displays. Above them, even the air was hung with baubles and banners. Voices were everywhere, laughing and exclaiming over the beauties and riches to be found, the clever crafts and ingenious arts. Voices were raised in song, and old friends met and shared their joy in the day, and in each other.

As they passed from stall to stall, Willie and Nick could hardly control their excitement. This was the day they had waited for so long, and it was even more than they had hoped for. They felt like children, bouncing from one delight to another.

In a quiet moment, Willie said to Nick, "I wish little Wolf could see all this. He loved warmth and abundance. He needed them so. It's a pity he can't be here now."

Nick said, "But he is here."

As the day drew to a close, everyone gathered in the great village hall for the evening ceremonies. All voices were raised in praise of the Springfest. The hall was hung with banners, and tables were laden with every kind of food that anyone could possibly want.

And when all had eaten their fill, it was time for Nick, the creator of the Springfest, to rise and speak to his friends.

"People of the Valley Beyond the World's Edge!" he began. "For a long time, we believed there was nothing beyond the mist and the mountains that surround us. But now we know better. And so it is both my duty and my joy to collect the many wonderful things that you have made with your hands and hearts, and bring them as the Valley's gifts to the people of the World, filling the sleigh the Raindeer will pull on Christmas Eve, this and every Christmastime!

"Some of you may have been wondering, why am I the one to do this thing! Well, once upon a time, as the saying goes, I was a child in that World. I remembered it as a terrible place—but then a little boy reminded me that it can also be a place filled with love. There are many ways we can show each other that love, as you, my dear friends, know very well. One of them is by giving a gift."

He held up an apple from the table.

"We are sending our best gifts to the World. But before we get too caught up in what our heads can plan and our hands can make, we should also remember that everything we make comes to us first as a gift: the gift of Nature.

"You see this simple apple! This is a gift of Nature. No human hands can make this wonderful thing. But my mother taught me that with my two hands, I can take Nature's gift and make one of my own."

With his knife, Nick cut the apple in half and held on high the Apple Star.

"The Apple Star: my gift to you, people of the Valley, a gift the earth gives to us, that we can give to each other. No hands can make it, but two hands can shape it, and all hands can take it."

As he turned to hand Willie the apple, Nick heard a roaring in his ears. It was the people in the hall, shouting with excitement:

"The Riddle! The Lost Riddle has been solved!"

And he realized what he had said.

Someone picked up a sack and spilled its contents on the table before him. Apples green and red and gold poured out before the people of the Valley.

No hands can make me
Two hands can shape me
All hands can take me

Nick cut open the fruit, and star after star after star lit the table and the shining faces of his friends.

And with one voice they cheered.

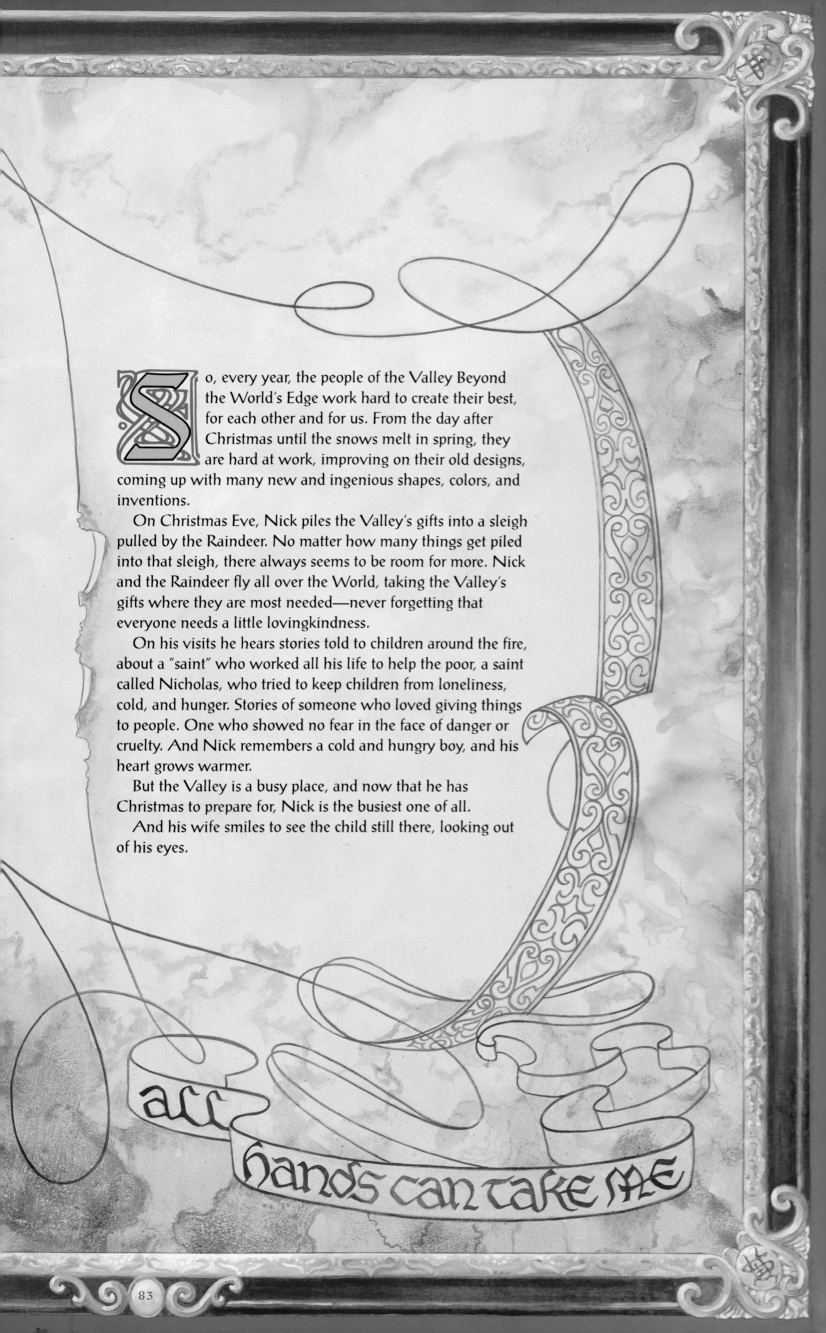

So, every year, the people of the Valley Beyond the World's Edge work hard to create their best, for each other and for us. From the day after Christmas until the snows melt in spring, they are hard at work, improving on their old designs, coming up with many new and ingenious shapes, colors, and inventions.

On Christmas Eve, Nick piles the Valley's gifts into a sleigh pulled by the Raindeer. No matter how many things get piled into that sleigh, there always seems to be room for more. Nick and the Raindeer fly all over the World, taking the Valley's gifts where they are most needed—never forgetting that everyone needs a little lovingkindness.

On his visits he hears stories told to children around the fire, about a "saint" who worked all his life to help the poor, a saint called Nicholas, who tried to keep children from loneliness, cold, and hunger. Stories of someone who loved giving things to people. One who showed no fear in the face of danger or cruelty. And Nick remembers a cold and hungry boy, and his heart grows warmer.

But the Valley is a busy place, and now that he has Christmas to prepare for, Nick is the busiest one of all.

And his wife smiles to see the child still there, looking out of his eyes.

all hands can take me

ACKNOWLEDGMENTS

Special recognition to
Michael Fragnito of Viking Studio Books.
Without his vision, our *St. Nicholas* would not
have happened. To the Viking Studio Books
editors and artisans—Barbara Williams, Amy
Hill, and Roni Axelrod—whose creative skills
guided this book's production; and to Martha
Schueneman, our editor, liaison, and friend.

In the beginning
the original book's concept was nudged along
by Doug Pheiffer and his publishing colleague,
Richard Bye.

Along the way
for providing some of the earliest inspiration for
our visual story, we sincerely thank Bob Walsh
and Bernie Russi; for his original design philo-
sophy, which still permeates these pages, Bill
Allen; our good friend Bernie Comer, whose open
workshop saved us many times; and John Larson.

The unwavering belief and good commonsense
of Cooper Edens, our eternal friend, who helped
us stay our course; Harold and Sandra Darling,
who provided insights into the publishing world;
Peter and Helen Neumeyer, who to this day are
our greatest source of storybook knowledge and

understanding; and Lou Corsaletti, who still believes in Santa Claus! Of special note, Claire Ondik, Dave Battey, and Bob Barnes, who took the time to pitch in when we needed them most.

A lift in time
Particular mention and gratitude to our good friend Ruth McIntyre, who inspires the project even today.

Day-to-day contributors
To those individuals who ask nothing but the opportunity to help, we acknowledge Sharon Larson of the North Bend Library and her staff, Helen Bonomi, Kathy Goble, and Patricia Simpson; the Snoqualmie Valley Historical Museum; the Vernell Candy Company of Bellevue, Washington.

And we thank Viola McCullough, Robert Bybee, and Sharon Mills, whose home interests and crafts provided reference for our work.

The St. Nicholas Church of Stein, Austria; the Salzburg Marionette Theater in Salzburg, Austria; the Vienna Rathaus for its inspiration; and *Vienna for being Vienna!*

Our model director
Georgia Kramer, who has been a well of inspiration and an endless source of studio models.

And finally . . .
Our Snoqualmie Valley models, those wonderful people who came into our studio— climbing into costume after costume—and worked so hard to make their characters authentic. We personally thank Bill Allen, Peter Barnes, Dave Battey, Robert Burhans, Dave and Sharon Caldwell, Don and Lynda Carlson, Betty Carmichael, Bernie and Gerrie Comer, Gail Cornett, Race Dillon, Bob Drake, Lee Dreyer, Dragen and Ilse Dujmovic, Katerina Fedor-White, Beau and Brittney Foster, Kathy Furulie, Caleb Garvin, Mike Gifford and his sons Matthew, Mark, and Nathan, Fred Hassel, Nick and Gayle Head, Ken Heuberger, Adi and Eva Hienzsch, Harold Hurn, Barney and Donna Kaplan, Anneliese Kellogg, Georgia Kramer, Joyce Littlejohn, George Macris, Amanda, Joshua, and Ryan Magnussen, Dick McConkey, Ruth McIntyre, Judy McNea, Michelle Melde, Nick and Magen Michaud, Larry Olson, Colin and Kelsey Parsons, Kyle and Ada Riley, Lee Riley, Mary Ann Rohrbach, Woodrow Ross, Louis Rowley, Mark Ruppert, Walt Rutledge, Brandon Sales, Chuck Schroeder, John Sheppard, Marvin and Phyllis Slaght, Daniel and Rachel Smith, Wes and Jean Stanley, LaTasha Stewart, Aaron, Joshua, and Katrina Styx, Angela and Terese Taklo, Holly Turner, Toby Van Bryce, Anthony Venera, Suzette Verzola, Howard and Florence Welborn, Chelsey and Shelby Westerlund, Marge Williams, and Jessica Wu.

Our warmest thanks to each one.

Ellen Kushner thanks the Burhans for their inspiration, the people of Viking for their encouragement, Julie Fallowfield for her never-ending battle with the Forces of Darkness, and Delia Sherman for her insight and support.